Phonobet

Phonemes are the sounds that make up every word we say. They appear in this book in **this font**. Pronounce these sounds as if they were in the middle of a word, not as separate letters! For example, **ng** should be pronounced like the sound at the end of 'sing'.

There are two sounds marked **th**:
one with your voice turned off like in 'thin',
and one with your voice turned on like in 'the'.
There are also two sounds marked **oo**:
the first as in 'book' and the second as in 'moon'.
zh refers to the sound in 'vision'.

Phono-bet

KATHY WEEDEN & KIM DRANE

I'm sure you've met the Alphabet, our very tidy friend,
with A at the beginning, and Z right at the end.

It's nice and neat and works a treat
for every writing need,
except for one small problem:
it's a little hard to read.

There are letters that behave themselves, with one main sound to each,

like D for dog and dinosaur and B for bat and beach.

But some are far more cunning like the A in catch and caught,

the O in owl and ox and oat, or U in funny thought.

A to Z

So is it just a muddled mess we have to learn by heart,
or does our good old Alphabet have friends who play a part?

Come and meet the Phonobet, a very handy twin:
a set of all the sounds you use when waggling your chin.

Beginning with the consonants:
they number twenty-four,
depending on your accent
maybe fewer, maybe more.

a B C D e F G H i J
K L M N o P Q
R S T u V W
X Y Z

f · th · s · sh · h are rustling trees,

v · th · z · zh: a hive of buzzing bees.

p · t · ch · k: a train along a track,

bridge

digger

BANG!

goat

bus

bongo

jazz

library

b · d · j · g:

drum, with a bang and a whack!

road

sweets

robot

yellow

win

w · l · r · y: the sound of robots talking,

m · n · ng: humming nannas going walking.

Moving on to vowels:
roughly twenty here in all,
your mouth and lips and
tongue in shapes,
big as well as small.

no!

a · e · i · o · u · oo

sound like monkeys, short and sweet,

corn

ball

shirt

car

barn

fern

grass

word

while **ar**, **or** and **er**
are zombies, groaning on the street.

A smiley pirate greets us: **ay** and **ee** and **igh** and **oy**.

But **ou** and **oe** and **oo**: that's a very grumpy boy!

Which leaves us with the random
smelly **eer** and **air** and **ure**,
from yucky, stinky words like earwax,
hair and fresh manure.

pear
deer
manure

captain

colour

iron

paper

uttoN

Besi

pencil

away

And just one more,
the sneaky **schwa**,
the shruggish **uh** that hides
in all the lazy bits of words
like button and besides.

BUTTON
AND
BESIDES

sister

So, once you know the Phonobet,
I'm certain that you'll find
a wacky world of wonder words
with sounds of every kind.
The sounds are yours to say and sing
and twist and taste and chew.

CLOUD
UMBRELLA
RAIN
MIRROR
DINO
EE
TREE
Hello
Greetings
MUSHROOMS
Yap!
Yap!
LA
FOX

And then, what should you do with them?
Well, that's up to you.

EXPLORING YOUR VOICE

Speaking may feel easy, but there are lots of things going on in your body to make it all happen. You use your lungs, throat, vocal cords, tongue, teeth, lips, nose, and all sorts of muscles to make each sound that comes out of your mouth. Each language uses a different set of sounds (also called phonemes). English uses around 44 sounds (depending on where you live). These sounds can be grouped into consonants and vowels.

Consonants

Consonants are sounds that are made by stopping the air coming out of your mouth in some way. You can:

- stop the air completely and make it pop out of your mouth, like **p** in pop
- let air out of hissy gaps, like **f** and **z** in fizz
- make it pop and hiss through your teeth, like the **ch** in chew

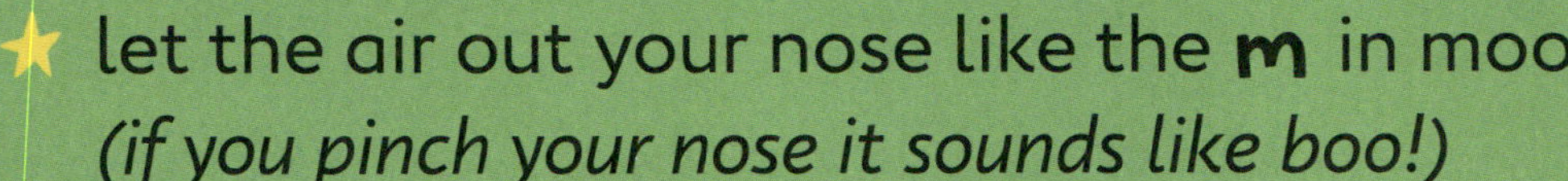

- let the air out your nose like the **m** in moo *(if you pinch your nose it sounds like boo!)*
- give the air small spaces to get out like **w** and **r** in worry

Voice On, Voice Off

Put your hand on your throat and say **ffff**. Now say **vvvv**. Did that feel different? Was your throat buzzing? Some sounds are like whispers, when your voice is turned off (vocal cords staying still), while others need your voice to be on (vocal cords vibrating).

Lips, Teeth and Tongue

Consonants also differ from each other depending on which part/s of the mouth you are using to stop the sound. Are you using your lips? Lips and teeth? Tongue and teeth? Tip of the tongue? Back of the tongue? Have a play around. Maybe you can come up with some new sounds you don't normally use!

VOICELESS

Hissing *(fricative)*
f in fun, **th** in thin, **s** in sun, **sh** in shoe, **h** in hat

Popping *(plosive)*
p in pop, **t** in toe, **k** in kite

Pop and Hiss *(affricate)*
ch in chew

VOICED

Hissing *(fricative)*
v in van, **th** in this, **z** in zoo, **zh** in beige

Popping *(plosive)*
b in bat, **d** in do, **g** in goo

Pop and Hiss *(affricate)*
j in jam

Humming *(nasal)*
m in mum, **n** in no, **ng** in sing

Small gap *(approximant)*
w in wet, **r** in ram, **l** in lolly, **y** in yak

Vowels

Vowels are made with your mouth open in different shapes. They can be tall or short shapes, wide or skinny shapes. Your tongue can be right at the back of your mouth, or almost poking out! The best way of exploring this is to stand in front of a mirror and make silly faces.

Beyond making shapes, vowels also differ by how long they are. They can be short and punchy like monkey sounds, or long like the groans of a zombie. They can also start in one shape and move to another. Can you make a sound that ends in a smile like in **hi** or **hay**? How about one that ends with your lips making a tiny circle like **ow**?

Short

a in apple, **e** in egg, **i** in ink, **o** in on, **u** in up,
oo in book, **uh** in the

Long and moving *(diphthongs)*

ar in car, **or** in corn, **er** in her, **ay** in hay,
ee in tree, **igh** in high, **oy** in boy,
ou in loud, **oe** in toe, **oo** in moon,
ure in cure, **air** in hair, **eer** in deer

How to Write a Sound

The sounds in this book appear in **a special font** and whichever spelling is most common or least confusing, but that isn't the only way to do it.

In the late nineteenth century, a group of language teachers got together to devise a set of symbols that could represent the sounds of all languages. The International Phonetic Alphabet was born. More than a hundred years later, it is still being used all over the world. You can look for it in your dictionary. Here is a secret message in the phonetic alphabet for you to decode:

kɐm ænd miːt ðə fɔnəbet
jʉː hæv dʒest ɹed ə siːkɹət mesədʒ

A World of Accents

The sounds in this book are based on Australian Standard English, but there are many other English accents. (Your accent is the way you pronounce words when you speak.)

All over the world, people speak English with accents that reflect their individual stories and identities.

You can start exploring how your accent is similar or different to others with these pairs of words. Do they sound the same or different when you say them? How about when your friends or people on television say them? Words that sound the same when you say them might sound different from each other when someone in or from another country says them.

bean/bin
cot/caught
witch/which
den/then
satin/Saturn
bud/bird
door/dough

her/hair
caught/court
paw/poor
tow/tour
snot/snort
voice/verse
hot/heart

book/buck
art/heart
look/Luke
toon/tune
fin/thin
wink/rink

Answer: Come and meet the Phonobet. You have just read a secret message.

FUN WITH SOUNDS!

Leaves in the Wind

Pick a nice big leaf (or cut one out of paper) and write or stick one of the tree sounds on to it (e.g. **f**). As one person gently rustles the leaf, everyone else makes that sound. As the leaf moves more, make the sound louder, but be sure to keep your voice turned off! Once you're ready, use more leaves to represent the other tree sounds: **th · s · sh · h**.

Insect Swarm

Use a puppet (or just your fingers!) to represent a bee flying high and low: **zzzzz**. As your bee flies high, see if you can get your voice to go high and squeaky too. When your bee flies low, make your bumbly bee buzz in a low rumbly voice. Can you do the same for the other bee sounds: **v · th · zh**?

Beat Box Train

Draw a train with carriages to represent the four train sounds. Make one of the sounds as you point to each carriage: **p · t · ch · k**, **p · t · ch · k**. As your train gets faster and faster, your sounds get faster and faster too. Can you slow down as your train goes up a hill, and speed up as you come down the other side? Don't forget to do a big train whistle when you get back to the station!

TREASURE HUNT

Here's a little treasure hunt. Dare to have some fun?
Take a look and you will find every sound but one.
Do you know which sound is missing?

Waltzing Matilda

A.B. 'Banjo' Paterson

Once a jolly swagman camped by a billabong
Under the shade of a coolabah tree,
And he sang as he watched and waited till his billy boiled,
'You'll come a-waltzing Matilda, with me.'

Chorus:

Waltzing Matilda, waltzing Matilda,
You'll come a-waltzing Matilda, with me,
And he sang as he watched and waited till his billy boiled,
'You'll come a-waltzing Matilda, with me.'

Down came a jumbuck to drink at that billabong,
Up jumped the swagman and grabbed him with glee,
And he sang as he shoved that jumbuck in his tucker bag,
'You'll come a-waltzing Matilda, with me.'

zh air igh ch oo i ure eer l sh th y f ou s j k b ar ay u

v uh e t oo

Chorus

Up rode the squatter, mounted on his thoroughbred.
Down came the troopers, one, two, and three.
'Whose is that jumbuck you've got in your tucker bag?
You'll come a-waltzing Matilda, with me.'

Chorus

Up jumped the swagman and sprang into the billabong.
'You'll never catch me alive!' said he.
And his ghost may be heard as you pass by that billabong:
'You'll come a-waltzing Matilda, with me.'

Chorus

er th r oe or oy w ng ee h g z

o q n m p d

Hint: It's a little obscure.

For Olivia, Callum and Ben, my joyful noise-makers. KW

Published by National Library of Australia Publishing
Canberra ACT 2600

ISBN: 9781922507471

The National Library of Australia acknowledges Australia's First Nations Peoples—the First Australians—as the Traditional Owners and Custodians of this land and gives respect to the Elders—past and present—and through them to all Australian Aboriginal and Torres Strait Islander people.

Publisher: Lauren Smith
Managing editor: Amelia Hartney
Editor: Helen Bethune Moore
Designer: Hannah Janzen
Image coordinator: Jemma Posch
Printed in China by Asia Pacific Offset on FSC®-certified paper.

Waltzing Matilda lyrics reflect Marie Cowan's 1903 version (nla.cat-vn2029534) of the A.B. 'Banjo' Paterson original, drafts of which are held by the National Library of Australia.
Page 39 image caption: Lionel Lindsay, *Swagman Walking with Dog*, 1939, nla.cat-vn2311324

Teachers' notes for this book are available at publishing.nla.gov.au/pages/teachers-notes.do.
Find out more about NLA Publishing at nla.gov.au/national-library-publishing.

A catalogue record for this book is available from the National Library of Australia

FSC
www.fsc.org
MIX
Paper | Supporting responsible forestry
FSC® C136333